Colby
the Coal mining bee

by Rebecca Tyler

illustrated by Alexandra Dan

Colby was a good bee.
He worked hard to make things better for his swarm.
Whenever the hive had a leak, he'd make repairs.

He also would harvest pollen, so that he and the other bees could make honey.

Sometimes, he'd visit the larvae in the nursery.
He would play with them and tell them stories.

He had a happy, productive life. But, sometimes he wondered if there wasn't more that he could do.

He was curious about the giant creatures that would arrive near his hive every morning. They didn't have wings and couldn't fly, but they were yellow and black, just like him!

Every day, they would go into a tunnel, and shortly afterwards, Colby would hear excited buzzing sounds.

Colby wondered: Were they giant bees? Did they find a new source of pollen in the tunnel?

He decided that he would follow the creatures and learn more. But, he had to ask the Queen Bee if he could take a few days off work.

"Excuse me, Queen Bee, may I follow the large, flightless bees into their tunnel and see what they are doing there?"

She thought for a moment. "Colby, I don't believe these creatures are large flightless bees. I think they are different animals entirely."

"But, your majesty, they are yellow and black, like us. They make buzzing noises, like us.

They go into their tunnel every day and return with large amounts of...I don't know what, but it could be pollen!" The Queen was quiet for a while.

"Very well, Colby," she finally said. "You may take a couple of days off work, and follow these creatures. There are 21,548 adult bees in the colony and they can gather pollen, and care for larvae, and repair the hive while you are gone."

Colby bowed and said Thank You.

Colby watched the creatures and knew what he needed to get. First, he needed a sharp tool, as he noticed that they all had sharp tools. So, he found a nice thorn.

Then, he needed a light to attach to his head.
So, he went to his friend, the Lightning Bug.

"Lightning Bug, may I borrow your light, so that I can follow some large, flightless bees into their dark hive?"
"Why, certainly you may borrow my light. I don't even use it anymore."*

*Only male lightning bugs have lights, which they use to attract mates.

Colby also noticed that each flightless bee would carry a bucket with lunch.
So, he also packed a lunch.

Finally, in the morning,
he was ready to go!

Confident that he would fit right in with the creatures, Colby bravely flew from behind the tree.
    He joined the line of giant, flightless bees as they walked into the tunnel.

Good morning!
A fine morning it is!

Colby followed them deep into their tunnel, and was happy that his friend let him borrow such a nice light.

The large, flightless bees then wasted no time, and started beating their tools against the wall. Colby found this...confusing.

But Colby knew it was important to seem natural. So he joined in, using his rose thorn to stab at the wall, not understanding why.

He noticed that the creatures were removing parts of the wall and dropping them into the cart.

Compared to the pieces the giants were pulling off the wall, his pieces were just tiny flecks.

But he added them to the cart, anyway.

Colby had to fly up high above the cart to avoid being hit by flying chunks of wall.
From a safe distance above, he would let his pieces fall.

The work was so hard!

He was happy when the creatures stopped
    to eat their lunch.
It gave him a chance
        to rest and to eat his lunch, too.

Before he could finish eating, it started again!
They were back at work!

Colby started working again, too. But he was so confused. Where was the pollen? What were they doing here? He decided to just ask.

He approached one of the large flightless bees. "Excuse me," Colby said. "I'm not complaining. But I do wonder what we're doing here. I'm experienced in honeycomb construction projects, but I've never worked to tear something down.

What is our goal in all of this?"

Then, swoosh!
The large, flightless bee batted Colby away!
Colby was barely able to avoid being squished
against the wall! He didn't even give Colby an answer,
not even a single bzzzz.

Colby continued to work, but he was more confused than ever.

By the end of the day, he was exhausted.
There was no sign that the day had been successful.
He would feel foolish explaining this to the Queen Bee.

Finally, the creatures started to gather their tools and they lined up to leave the tunnel, carting their silly, pointless collection of the pieces of the wall. The creatures acted like the cart was valuable, yet it contained no pollen, no food... nothing worthwhile to his hive! Colby had never worked so hard in his life, and it was for nothing!

The creatures were gone. The food was still there. They simply left this treasure behind, on the floor! Did they do this every day? Colby couldn't believe his eyes. He had to go to his hive and tell the swarm right away.

He woke his friends up from bed, and excitedly told them about the amazing, delicious food awaiting them.

Colby used his headlight to lead his swarm to the priceless treasure.

Seeing the food, none of his friends could believe their eyes!

The bees had a wonderful party, and they ate more sweets than they ever imagined. Colby earned the respect of all of the bees in the hive.

His hard work and creative thinking paid off!

In real life, Colby would actually be a girl bee. Boy bees are very rare, sometimes as few as 100 of them can live in a hive of 20,000 or more.

There really are Queen bees. Only one Queen lives in each hive, and is guarded and provided for by all of the other bees. She is the only one in the colony that lays eggs. Bees can have many different jobs over their lives. Nurse Bees make jelly to give to the grubs. Builder Bees work to construct hives. Foraging bees work outside the hive, bringing back pollen to make honey. Guard bees stay by the hive to protect it from intruders. A bee can have all of these jobs over the course a lifetime.

In real life, Colby wouldn't use maps to find pollen, but would do something called a "waggle dance."
When a bee finds a source of pollen, she goes back into the hive and does a dance that communicates the direction and distance of the flowers, using the sun as a reference point.

Throughout history, people have enjoyed honey. There are cave drawings of people looking for honey, and as long ago as Ancient Egypt, people were beekeepers.

In recent years, bees have been dying in large numbers, as a result of a mysterious problem called "colony collapse disorder". No one is entirely certain what is wrong. Solving this problem is extremely important as bees pollinate up to a third of plants.

35647098R00025

Made in the USA
Lexington, KY
19 September 2014